PUFFIN BOOKS

SUPERPOWERS

THE TUSKED TERROR

Books by Alex Cliff
SUPERPOWERS series

SUPER POWERS

THE TUSKED TERROR

ALEX CLIFF

ILLUSTRATED BY LEO HARTASS

PUFFIN

PUFFIN BOOKS

Published by the Penguin Group
Penguin Books Ltd, 80 Strand, London WC2R 0RL, England
Penguin Group (USA) Inc., 375 Hudson Street, New York, New York 10014, USA
Penguin Group (Canada), 90 Eglinton Avenue East, Suite 700, Toronto, Ontario, Canada M4P 2Y3
(a division of Pearson Penguin Canada Inc.)
Penguin Ireland, 25 St Stephen's Green, Dublin 2, Ireland (a division of Penguin Books Ltd)
Penguin Group (Australia), 250 Camberwell Road, Camberwell, Victoria 3124, Australia
(a division of Pearson Australia Group Pty Ltd)
Penguin Books India Pvt Ltd, 11 Community Centre, Panchsheel Park,
New Delhi – 110 017, India
Penguin Group (NZ), 67 Apollo Drive, Rosedale, North Shore 0632, New Zealand
(a division of Pearson New Zealand Ltd)
Penguin Books (South Africa) (Pty) Ltd, 24 Sturdee Avenue, Rosebank,
Johannesburg 2196, South Africa

Penguin Books Ltd, Registered Offices: 80 Strand, London WC2R 0RL, England

puffinbooks.com

Published 2007
1

Set in Bembo
Typeset by Palimpsest Book Production Limited, Grangemouth, Stirlingshire
Made and printed in England by Clays Ltd, St Ives plc

British Library Cataloguing in Publication Data
A CIP catalogue record for this book is available from the British Library

ISBN: 978–0–141–32136–3

To Innes and Alexander, for having to put up with their older brothers being in these books

CONTENTS

JUST IMAGINE . . .

a crumbling castle on a hillside. It is early morning. Streaks of pale light spread across the sky as the sun begins to rise. In the arched doorway of the castle's single remaining tower a woman can be seen. She is much taller than a normal woman and a cloak of brown-grey feathers swirls around her shoulders. It is the evil goddess Juno.

'The boys are winning, Juno,' the superhero Hercules says from his prison inside the tower walls. 'You have set them three tasks in the last three days. So far they have completed every task and returned three of my superpowers to me.'

Juno swings round. 'I know that!' she snaps. 'But remember, you cannot escape until you have all seven of your powers back. The boys have four more tasks ahead of them, and today they face this . . .'

Juno claps her hands together. When she opens them, a ball is cupped within her palms. White fire seems to swirl inside it. Slowly the fire in the ball clears to show a picture of an enormous wild boar the size of a rhinoceros with two sharp tusks. It is pacing around a rocky mountain lair in a wooded clearing; its last meal lies at its feet. The boar's muscles ripple and its snout wrinkles to reveal vicious teeth that drip with saliva as it roots in delight at its fresh prey.

Juno carries the ball into the tower. A square of stones is missing in the far wall. Hercules looks out through it. His hair is long and fair, his face lined but noble.

'Do you remember capturing the Giant Boar of Erymanthia?' Juno asks, holding out the ball for him to see.

Hercules looks at the boar grimly. 'I remember it well.'

'To win back another of your superpowers the boys must bring the Giant Boar into the castle grounds,' Juno says. 'For today I have moved its lair from the Land of the Gods to Saddleback Mountain just over there.' She nods through the tower doorway to the neighbouring wooded mountain to the west of the castle. 'It is the toughest

task yet. Those two boys will *never* succeed.'

Hercules stares at her. 'Do not underestimate them, Juno. They have already captured the sabre-toothed lion, killed the Nine-Headed River Monster and cleaned the impossibly dirty stables.'

'By luck!' Juno's voice snaps like an icicle cracking. 'Today I know they will fail!' She throws the ball in the air and it vanishes with a bang. 'And then it will not just be you and they who are sorry.'

Hercules looks at her warily. After

centuries of fighting he knows the goddess well. 'What are you planning, Juno?'

Juno twirls a lock of her long brown hair. 'I think it is time for those boys to prove whether they are real heroes, and as we both know, true heroes save others not just themselves.'

'No, Juno!' Hercules exclaims. 'You cannot put the responsibility of saving other people on two eight-year-old boys!'

A smile spreads across Juno's face. 'You should know by now that I can do anything I want, Hercules!' She clicks her fingers. The stones instantly close over Hercules' face, shutting him back into his prison again. 'Anything!' the goddess whispers mockingly.

She claps her hands. There is a thunderclap and she vanishes. As the echo of the thunder fades a hawk swoops out of the tower. It flies up into the sky and heads like an arrow towards the neighbouring mountain.

CHAPTER ONE

HOW TO CATCH A BOAR

Finlay Yates looked down the path that sloped from his garden shed to the front gate. How close could he get to the gate on his bike today? There was only one way to find out!

Jumping on to his bike, he pedalled at full speed down the slope. As he reached the gate he jammed the back brake on full and swung his weight to the side. The bike skidded to a sideways stop on the driveway, throwing up a wave of gravel.

'Wicked!' Finlay grinned. He reckoned he was only about ten centimetres away from the gate.

'Mum'll kill you if she catches you doing that!' Jasmine, Finlay's twelve-year-old sister, warned as she wheeled her own bike sensibly down the path. 'You know she says it's dangerous!'

Finlay grinned. 'So?' A picture of the giant dung beetles he and his best friend, Max, had faced the day before jumped into his mind. Now they had *really* been dangerous! And then there had been the river monster the day before and the sabre-toothed lion the day before that. Wondering what Jasmine would say if he told her about the terrifying monsters he and Max had been fighting for the last three days, he ran his bike back up the slope to try again.

'Don't!' Jasmine frowned.

But Finlay was already whizzing down the slope. This time he was a split second from smashing into the gate.

'Finlay!' Jasmine exclaimed as gravel hit her legs.

Just then Max came cycling along the road. 'How many centimetres?' he called over the gate.

'Three,' Finlay replied, looking at the distance from his front tyre to the bottom of the gate.

'Cool!' Max grinned.

Jasmine rolled her eyes despairingly. 'Oh, please tell me you two aren't going to be hanging around here all day, annoying me.'

'Nah, we're going to the castle,' Finlay replied.

'The castle!' Jasmine said, looking suddenly interested. 'Are you still looking for those hidden dungeons?'

Finlay frowned, a bit puzzled, and then suddenly remembered what Jasmine was talking about. Three days ago he and Max had gone to the castle to try and find its secret underground dungeons. However, before they could even start looking they'd found the superhero Hercules imprisoned in the tower wall. He'd been put there by the evil goddess Juno after a great battle in the castle grounds. She had stripped him of his superpowers, placing them in the stones around the castle gatehouse entrance. Ever since then Max and Finlay had forgotten about the dungeons and had been trying to help Hercules get his superpowers back.

Juno enjoyed watching humans die and so she had struck a deal with the two boys. Each day she would set them an almost impossible task and they could choose one of Hercules' superpowers to help them. If they completed the task by sunset then the

power returned to Hercules; if they failed then the superpower would be lost forever. So far Max and Finlay hadn't failed. In the last three days they had managed to restore Hercules' powers of speed, strength and size-shifting. There were four powers left now – accuracy, agility, defence and courage – and Finlay and Max intended to win them all back for the superhero.

'Well?' Jasmine said, waiting for an answer.

'Um . . . yes,' Finlay said quickly. 'We're still looking for the dungeons.'

Max backed him up. 'Yeah, looking and looking.'

'It would be great if you found them,' Jasmine told them. 'The castle's really interesting. We did a project on it last year at school. Did you know there was once an underground tunnel that ran from the castle to a nearby mountain? It was built so that people could escape if the castle was besieged, but no one knows where the entrances are now. You could try and find them too.'

Usually Finlay would have been really interested in the thought of a secret tunnel but right now he had more important things to think about – like the Giant Boar that Juno had said he and Max had to capture that day!

Max seemed to be thinking the same thing. 'We'd better get to the castle,' he said, shooting Finlay a meaningful look.

'I'd better go too. I've got a riding lesson this morning then Natasha's coming back for the day,' Jasmine said, getting on to her bike. 'See you later.'

As soon as she had cycled away Finlay turned to Max. 'Have you got everything we decided?'

Max nodded. 'Hammer, net and rope,' he replied quickly.

Finlay ran over the idea he'd told Max about on the phone the night before. 'So we find the boar, I lasso it then knock it out by throwing a hammer at its head, then while it's knocked out we tie it up with the net and drag it back to the castle.'

Max nodded. 'Yep, and you choose the superpower of deadly accuracy to help you.'

Finlay felt a rush of excitement. This task was going to be OK. They had a plan. They had weapons. All they needed was the superpower. 'Cool!' he said. 'Let's go and find us a pig!'

As he wheeled his bike through the gate the front door of the house opened and Mrs Yates came out with Finlay's three-year-old sister, Sophie. Mrs Yates saw the tyre marks on the gravel and frowned. 'Finlay, have you been skidding on the drive?'

Finlay tried to look innocent. 'Me? Never!' He quickly opened the gate before his mum could question him any further. 'Bye, Mum! We're going to the castle.'

Mrs Yates nodded. 'I'll be out on a playgroup trip with Sophie until this afternoon. We're going to Saddleback Mountain Nature Trail for a picnic

lunch there.' Sophie, wearing bright-red wellies, and with her fair hair in bunches, skipped down to the gate.

'Come on, Sophie. We don't want to be late,' Mrs Yates called.

'Neither do we,' Max muttered to Finlay.

The superpowers could only be taken from the gatehouse wall for twenty minutes every morning just as the sun's rays fell on the stones. If the boys weren't there to take the power at the right time they would lose their chance for the day.

Finlay jumped on to his bike. 'Let's go!'

'How's your leg?' Finlay asked Max as they cycled up the overgrown path to the castle.

The day before, a giant beetle had attacked Max when they'd been cleaning out some stables with an impossible amount of poo in them.

'It really hurts,' he replied. 'How's your shoulder?'

'That hurts too,' Finlay said. The day before that, the Nine-Headed River Monster had stabbed him on his left shoulder with one of its fangs. In fact, every day since they had started doing Juno's tasks either he or Max had got injured in some way. It was always the person with the superpower who got injured and the wounds always ended up looking strangely like the symbol of the superpower on the gatehouse wall.

What was going to happen today? A shiver ran down Finlay's spine at the thought but he quickly pushed it away.

Leaving their bikes by the bridge that led across the moat, Finlay and Max scrambled through the ruined gatehouse and into the castle's inner keep. The four remaining symbols were glowing in the stones around the arched entrance of the gatehouse – an arrow, a stag, a lion and a shield. On the day they had first met Hercules there had been seven pictures there, but every time the boys took a superpower its symbol disappeared from the wall.

'Boys!' Hercules' voice echoed across the grass. When the sun shone on the superpower symbols in the morning, the stones around Hercules' face crumbled away for twenty minutes. It was Juno's way of taunting him – he could see his superpowers shining brightly but he was powerless to get to them. For the rest of the day the stones re-formed, encasing Hercules in the darkness of the wall.

'Hi, Hercules!' Finlay said, running across the keep.

Hercules spoke urgently. 'The Giant Boar of Erymanthia is waiting for you on Saddleback Mountain, boys. You must be quick! People are in danger. It will charge down the mountainside and kill anyone it meets.'

Finlay's mouth felt dry. 'It's on Saddleback Mountain?'

Hercules nodded.

Max looked at Finlay in alarm. 'But that's where Sophie's going with your mum.'

Finlay nodded, his heart pounding like a hammer in his chest. The boar would attack the children if it came across them!

'Do you have a plan?' Hercules asked quickly.

'Fin's going to use the power of deadly accuracy,' Max stammered. 'We're going to lasso the boar with some rope, knock it out by throwing a hammer at its head, then tie it up in a net.' As he explained the plan, above their heads a hawk circled slowly round the tower.

'You have thought of a good plan,' Hercules said approvingly. 'The boar is savage but stupid and the power of

accuracy will enable you to capture it. But you must be quick. There is no time to waste!'

Finlay's thoughts were racing. He had to get the superpower so he could help his mum and Sophie and all the other children and adults too! He ran across the castle keep. The symbols glowed brightly. His eyes fixed on the arrow – the symbol of accuracy. As soon as he touched it the superpower would flow into him and they could go and stop the boar.

He reached out his hand but just then there was a harsh cry from above and something swooped down in front of him in a blur of brown-grey feathers. For a moment Finlay caught a glimpse of a hooked beak and sharp talons. He gasped and tried to stop. His foot caught on a stone, and he stumbled forward. His hands reached out instinctively to save him from crashing into the wall.

As his finger hit the stones he felt a rush of warmth into his left arm. He looked at the wall. He was touching the shield and not the arrow! 'No,' he gasped as energy flooded into him. 'I've chosen the wrong superpower!'

CHAPTER TWO

MAGIC SHIELDS

Finlay felt the stone turn cold beneath his hand. The shield symbol had vanished from the wall. He swung round. 'It's all gone wrong!' he exclaimed.

'It was that bird!' Max cried. 'It made you stumble!'

'Juno!' Hercules roared from the tower.

High overhead the hawk cawed mockingly.

'I didn't see it coming,' Finlay said, racing back to Max and Hercules in dismay. 'I just tripped. How are we going to capture the boar with the superpower of defence? What is the power of defence anyway?'

'Defence is one of the more magical powers. It allows you to create magical barriers that can protect you or anyone else from harm,' Hercules replied. 'You will need my shield in order to channel the superpower.'

'Your shield!' echoed Finlay.

'Yes,' Hercules said. 'You remember how you found my sword when you had to fight the Nine-Headed River Monster?'

Finlay knew he'd never forget the time he'd reached into a hole in the wall and felt the stones crumbling around his hand as his fingers had closed on the hilt of Hercules' heavy sword. He nodded.

'My shield is hidden in the same way. Find a hole near my left hand,' Hercules said to him. 'If you reach in, the superpower will guide you.'

Finlay and Max scanned the wall. There were quite a few holes where stones had fallen out. One particularly large hole caught Max's eye. 'I bet it's that one,' he pointed out.

Finlay stuck his hand into the hole. The stones felt cold and rough. He reached in deeper and deeper. There was gritty sand beneath his fingers and then suddenly he felt something else. Something made of metal. 'I think I've found it!'

The stones around his arm began to crumble. A circular hole formed.

'Look!' Max breathed, as they saw a glint of silver in the darkness of the hole.

The shield was very heavy and

Finlay pulled it out with difficulty. Its front was engraved with pictures of strange beasts and at the back was a leather strap.

'Try it on!' Hercules urged Finlay.

Finlay hesitated. The shield weighed a ton! He didn't think he'd be able to lift it but he knew he had to try. He slipped his arm through the strap and gasped. The weight seemed to vanish from the shield. Suddenly it felt as light as if it were made of plastic. Finlay swung it up. He could hold it easily.

'It's magic!' he said. 'It's gone really light.'

'It is part of the superpower,' Hercules explained. 'You will be able to carry the shield without feeling its weight and use it to cast magical barriers.'

'How do I do that?' Finlay asked eagerly.

'Hold up the shield,' Hercules instructed him. 'Think about a magical barrier and where you would like it to be and say "Shield me" in your thoughts.'

Finlay swung the shield up and looked at the air in front of him. *Shield me*, he thought.

A shimmering silvery disc swirled out of the centre of the shield and glowed in the air about a metre away. It looked like one side of a bubble, its translucent surface reflecting a rainbow of light. Finlay tried moving the metal shield and the magic barrier moved too.

'That's it!' exclaimed Hercules. 'If you draw deeply enough on the superpower

that is now inside you then nothing will be able to pass through it.'

'Wow! Let's test it!' said Max, picking up a stone.

'You must keep the barrier strong with your mind,' Hercules told Finlay.

'You ready?' Max asked.

Finlay nodded and Max chucked the stone at him.

Shield me, Finlay thought.

As the stone reached the magic shimmering disc it bounced back as if it had hit a trampoline.

Max had to duck quickly to avoid being hit by it as it rebounded at him.

'Wow!'

Hercules smiled at Finlay. 'Very good.'

'Let's try something bigger!' Max said eagerly. He hurried outside. A few seconds later he returned, heaving a rock the size of a rugby ball in his arms. 'Let's see what happens when I chuck this!' he panted.

'Keep concentrating,' Hercules said quickly to Finlay. 'The heavier the object, the harder it is to create a barrier that will hold it back.'

Max hoicked up the boulder.

'You must use your mind to draw on the power,' Hercules went on. 'You must . . .'

'Hi-yaa!' Max yelled and he chucked the boulder as hard as he could at Finlay.

This is easy, thought Finlay. *Shield me!* He waited for the boulder to bounce off the magic shield.

'Argh!' he yelled as the big rock shot through the shimmering circle and flew straight at his head.

Throwing Hercules' shield up just in time, he managed to protect himself. The rock banged into the metal, almost knocking Finlay to the ground with its weight.

'What happened there?' he gasped as he staggered backwards.

'Your shield was not strong enough,' Hercules answered. 'It takes practice to learn how to hold off greater threats.'

'But we haven't got time!' Finlay said.

'What are we going to do? I can't even keep out a rock, let alone a giant boar!'

'Don't worry. We'll find a way to stop it,' Max told him.

Hercules looked at Max. 'You must be careful, boy. The boar is savage and its teeth and tusks are razor sharp. It hates noise, people and other animals – particularly other giant boars. Its brain is small, but its strength is massive. Maybe you should stay hidden.'

'No way!' Max exclaimed. 'We're in this together, aren't we, Fin?'

'Until the end,' Finlay joked in a fake movie-trailer voice. But at the same time he shot Max a grateful look. He didn't want Max to get hurt but he *really* didn't want to face the boar alone.

Hercules looked worried. 'You will

need a carefully thought-out plan. Now let me think . . .'

Finlay hurried to the doorway of the tower. In the distance he could see the wooded slopes of Saddleback Mountain. He imagined his mum and Sophie getting out of the car and setting off to the nature trail with the rest of the playgroup. He swung round. 'There isn't time to think. Come on, Max! We need to get to the mountain and stop that boar!'

CHAPTER THREE

THE MOUNTAIN LAIR

'Wait!' Hercules exclaimed. 'You cannot just go charging off to meet the Giant Boar. You need a plan.'

'We'll think of one on the way,' Finlay replied impatiently, swinging the shield over his shoulder as he ran out of the tower. 'We have to go!'

'Maybe we *should* stay and plan what we're going to do,' Max said hesitantly.

'No!' Finlay exclaimed. 'We have to go now!'

To his relief Max nodded and ran after him. 'See you later, Hercules!' he called as he caught up easily with Finlay.

'Boys!' Hercules shouted. 'It is madness to go unprepared! You are putting yourselves in terrible danger. Come back and . . .'

His voice cut off as the stones suddenly re-formed around his face.

Finlay and Max kept on running.

'How are we going to get to the mountain?' Max said as they scrambled through the gatehouse and ran to their bikes. 'I guess it's not far across the fields.'

'But there's no path,' Finlay replied, panting as he tried to keep up with Max, who was much faster at running than him. 'And the fields are really muddy. If we go that way we'll have to push our bikes and it'll take ages. It'll be much quicker cycling through the village and going up to the mountain car park.'

Max nodded and, jumping on their bikes, they cycled down the hill. The bikes bounced over the rough ground; loose stones and soil flew up into the air. Seeing the road just ahead of them Finlay slammed on his brakes. His bike skidded round and the shield banged on his back. Max only just managed to avoid crashing into him.

'No cars coming!' he gasped, checking the road. 'Saddleback Mountain's this way! Come on!'

They set off as fast as they could.

The narrow road twisted and turned out of the village and into the hills. Soon Finlay and Max were both red in the face and gasping for breath but they knew they couldn't slow down.

Finlay saw a sign up ahead: *Saddleback Mountain Car Park*.

'We're here!' he shouted, swinging into the small road. The car park was spread out before them. With a sick jolt Finlay saw his mum's car with

Sophie's car seat in the back.

'Look! That must be the playgroup!' Max exclaimed. He pointed to the main path that led out of the car park up the mountain. Just disappearing round the first bend was a group of young children, some skipping happily along the path, others being pushed along in buggies. The parents and playgroup helpers were chatting brightly as they shepherded the children along.

Finlay looked up the mountain into the trees. Somewhere near the jagged top the Giant Boar would be preparing to charge down the mountainside. A wave of helplessness swept over him. How could they ever hope to stop it?

'Maybe we should just tell the

grown-ups about the boar,' he said desperately.

'They'll never believe us!' Max said. 'They'll think we're making it up. We'll just end up arguing with them for ages.'

Finlay knew he was right. They'd waste precious time if they tried to convince the playgroup leaders to stop the trip because of a giant boar. There was no way round it. They had to find the boar and prevent it from coming down the mountain. 'Come on,' he said grimly, cycling faster. Max followed him up the path. 'Have you thought of a plan yet?'

'No,' Finlay replied. 'I guess I try and cast a magic barrier to stop it coming down the mountain.'

They glanced at each other. They

knew they were both thinking the same thing. If Finlay hadn't managed to cast a barrier strong enough to stop a boulder, how could he possibly hope to cast one that was strong enough to stop the Giant Boar?

Pushing the worry to the back of their minds, they focused on cycling.

To their relief the playgroup had turned off the path for a while to poke around in a small stream and so they managed to get by without being spotted. Finlay wasn't sure quite how he'd explain to his mum why he and Max were in the woods, let alone why he had a large silver shield swung over his shoulder.

They cycled on – past the nature trail, past the glittering waterfall that fell over a rocky ledge into a stream beside the path, past the picnic area and finally past Old John's Grave – a strange deep pit near the top of the mountain. It wasn't really a grave – that was just a local nickname. Finlay remembered how

he and Max had used to pretend the place was haunted. He wished that the Giant Boar was just pretend too. What was it going to be like? Words Hercules had used kept popping into his mind. *Savage . . . its teeth and tusks are razor sharp . . . its strength is massive . . .*

They reached the end of the main track. A few small trails wound upwards through the trees that covered the top of the mountain.

Max braked to a stop. 'How are we going to find the boar?' he asked, looking round uncertainly.

'I'm not sure,' Finlay replied. He dropped his bike at the side of the path and, gripping the shield, walked a few paces into the trees. 'Juno didn't tell us where its lair was.'

A loud grunting noise suddenly rang out from near the mountain top. The leaves of the nearby trees trembled and the ground shook as if something very big and very fierce was pounding and scraping at the forest floor.

'Maybe that was because she knew she didn't need to,' Max said slowly.

Finlay's skin prickled. 'What do we do?' he whispered. 'Go and find it?'

Neither of them moved.

A loud angry roar rang out through the trees.

Max gulped. 'That sounds more like a lion than a boar!'

Finlay thought of his mum and Sophie and tightened his grip on Hercules' shield. 'Come on!' He walked bravely forward.

'Look!' Max said, pointing ahead of them. Trees and bushes had been crushed and stamped on and a trail of fresh blood could be seen on the path. Bits of matted brown hair were caught on the broken branches around them.

Finlay felt sick but he forced himself to make a joke so as to feel better. 'Looks like the boar's been having quite a party. Shame we have to crash it.'

'I'd sooner crash *into* it – with a Sherman tank!' Max said.

They exchanged shaky grins.

The path continued to wind upwards until they reached a clearing.

'There!' Finlay hissed.

At the far side of the clearing was a rocky lair and a small stream. In front of the rocks was the Giant Boar. It looked as big as a car and had small mean eyes and a sparse brown coat covering its massive bulky body. Two sharp bloodstained tusks protruded from its snout. It pawed at the ground,

sending mud and pine needles flying into the air. As the boys watched, it swung its head from side to side and grunted savagely.

'How are we going to stop *that*?' Max whispered.

The boar took a few paces down the hill, revealing a big pile of bones – the remains of its last dinner. Suddenly it stopped and scented the air. Its tiny eyes gleamed and, throwing back its head, it gave a throaty roar. It began to charge towards the path.

A picture of Sophie and his mum flashed in front of Finlay's eyes. He had to stop it! Racing out into the clearing, he held up the shield.

Shield me, he thought desperately. *Shield me! Shield me!*

Seeing him, the boar skidded to a stop with a surprised grunt. At the same time a silvery light swirled from the centre of Hercules' shield and formed a giant disc in the air between the boar and Finlay.

Finlay had a horrible vision of the rock Max had thrown sailing through the last magic barrier he'd cast. Would this barrier be any stronger? A shiver of fear ran down his spine as he looked into the boar's savage eyes.

The Giant Boar hesitated and then snarled with rage and began to charge straight towards him and the magic shield!

CHAPTER FOUR

ANOTHER SCAR!

'Fin!' gasped Max.

The Giant Boar pounded down the slope, its mouth wrinkling back to reveal its yellow teeth.

Shield me! Finlay thought desperately.

The thundering of the boar's feet drowned out the frantic banging of his heart as the boar hit the disc dead centre. The magic barrier bent like the underneath of a trampoline but to Finlay's amazement and relief, it didn't break. The boar was flung backwards.

'You did it!' Max exclaimed from the bushes at the edge of the clearing. 'You stopped it, Finlay!'

The boar got to its feet. It lowered its head and prepared to charge at the disc again.

'It's coming back!' Finlay yelled.

The boar charged again, even faster. As it hit the shield, it was thrown back once more but not so far this time. The shield seemed to be weakening. The boar grunted and attacked the disc with its tusks, swiping its head from side to side. The shield began to rip.

'Argh!' Finlay yelled.

The shield disintegrated, turning into

silver wisps that floated up into the sky. The Giant Boar gave a triumphant squeal and looked menacingly at Finlay.

'Run, Fin!' Max yelled.

Finlay ran for his life. He charged to the nearest tree. The boar was heavy and slow to pick up speed and by the time it reached the tree trunk Finlay was hauling himself into the branches. But he still wasn't quite quick enough. The boar slashed at his legs.

'Ow!' Finlay cried as he felt one of the tusks slice at his left ankle. Grabbing the branch above him he pulled himself up out of the boar's reach. He looked down at his leg. The boar's tusk had ripped straight through his jeans and socks. Blood dribbled from the cut.

'Are you OK?' Max yelled. He'd shinned up a nearby tree for safety.

'It got me!' Fin exclaimed as the boar circled beneath him.

A drop of blood fell to the forest floor. The boar snuffled at it and snorted in delight. Its eyes narrowed and it backed off to prepare for a run at the tree.

Shield me! Finlay thought, holding out the shield as the boar began its charge.

A new disc immediately spun out. The boar crashed into it and was thrown back. Shaking itself, it got to its feet and tried again.

'We've got to do something, Max!' Finlay exclaimed. 'The barriers aren't strong enough to hold it back!' As he spoke the boar began to rip the second shield to smithereens with its tusks. 'If it goes down the mountain and meets the playgroup . . .' He broke off to concentrate on casting another magic barrier.

Max gulped. The thought of the boar charging into all those children was horrible. They had to stop it from going down the mountain. But how?

Unless . . .

An idea exploded into his head.

'Fin! What about instead of stopping the boar going down the mountain, we stop the playgroup from coming up?'

'Good one!' said Finlay, trying to concentrate on the barrier he was casting. 'But how do we do that?'

Max wracked his brains. It was usually Fin who came up with good ideas. What could he think of that might stop the boar? Maybe they could put something across the path so the playgroup would turn round. A tree trunk perhaps? But he and Fin would never be able to move a tree trunk. They needed something light enough that they could shift but that would stop the children. *Think*, Max told himself desperately. *Come on! Think!*

His eyes fell on the stream that flowed down the mountain, eventually becoming the waterfall. Water!

Of course!

'You could redirect the waterfall!' he burst out to Finlay. 'If you cast an invisible barrier up where the water starts to fall, it'll spill out all over the path instead of into the rocky pool. With all that water blocking the way the playgroup will have to turn round!'

'Yeah!' Finlay exclaimed. 'That's a brilliant idea!' A thought struck him. 'But how do I hold the boar off here *and* get to the waterfall?'

'I could distract the boar,' Max said, trying to ignore the wicked glint in the

Giant Boar's eye as it prepared to charge again. Cupping his hands to his mouth like a megaphone Max suddenly made a grunting noise just like the boar.

Finlay looked at him in astonishment.

'Remember what Hercules said!' Max shouted.

Suddenly Finlay got it. Of course! Hercules had told them that giant boars really hated other giant boars.

The boar had frozen as soon as it had heard the noise. Now it was looking round suspiciously.

Max grunted again. The boar gave an angry squeal. It galloped protectively to its lair and began to stamp around as if searching for another boar.

'It's working!' Max called to Finlay.

'I bet I can keep it here for a while. You go!'

It seemed to be their only chance.

'OK!' Finlay waited till the boar was looking away then climbed quickly down the tree. 'See you later!' he hissed.

He ran through the trees to where they'd left their bikes. Max leant back against the trunk of the tree and, cupping his hands to his mouth, began to make some more grunting noises.

The boar charged down the slope and crashed into the tree next to Max's as if it thought another boar was hiding behind it. The tree shook and bent as the boar gouged great gashes in the trunk with its tusks. Max gulped and tightened his grip on the branch he was sitting on. Suddenly he felt very alone . . .

Finlay flew down the path on his bike. Was he going to be in time? What if the playgroup had already reached the waterfall? What if he couldn't cast a strong enough shield to deflect the water?

He saw the waterfall in front of him. There was no one anywhere near it. The children must still be on their way

up the path. Finlay felt a rush of relief. Skidding to a stop he jumped off his bike with the shield. He had to be quick!

The stream of water fell over a rocky cliff into a pool beneath. He needed to get round the other side of the pool, so he could project a barrier under the lip of the cliff. When the water hit the barrier it would hopefully bounce towards the path instead of falling into the pool. He began to scramble over the wet rocks, wishing he was as strong and fast as Max. The water splashed at his trainers and jeans. His wounded ankle stung, but he ignored the pain. All he could think about was getting to the other side and casting a shield.

He heard the faint sound of children's laughter echoing up the track. It sounded as if the playgroup was nearly at the waterfall. Everything depended upon him.

I can do this, he thought. He took a determined breath. *I have to!*

CHAPTER FIVE

THE WATERFALL

Ducking behind a large boulder for cover Finlay held up Hercules' shield.

A shining disc swirled out of it and shimmered in the air in front of him. Focusing on it Finlay tilted the shield in his hand until it was parallel to the ground. The magic shield followed the movement until it looked like a giant, near-invisible plate hovering in the air.

Now, Finlay thought, *just to get it under the water . . .*

Finlay willed the magic barrier towards the waterfall. The disc slowly began to move through the air. *Further*, Finlay thought, *further . . .*

And suddenly it was there! It moved under the rocky lip of the waterfall. The water hit it and bounced upwards as if it had hit a solid barrier. It sprayed everywhere including all over Finlay. Spluttering in surprise, he quickly tilted the shield in his hand at a slight angle away from him. The shimmering barrier shifted too.

'Yes!' Finlay breathed in triumph as the water splashed to the other side, falling straight on to the footpath and running down the path in a rapidly moving stream. Still holding the barrier in place Finlay glanced towards the path. The playgroup children were just coming round the bend. He spotted Sophie skipping along with her friend Isabel. And there was his mum and the other adults.

The group stopped with gasps of surprise as they saw the water flowing down the path towards them. Young toddlers were quickly scooped up. The older children squealed with delight and ran forward to jump in the water.

'Look at the waterfall!' Finlay heard Ann, one of the playgroup leaders, exclaim. 'It's falling on the path!'

'How on earth is it doing that?' Mrs Yates said.

Luckily there was so much spray that

it hid the shield and the adults were quickly distracted by the excited children.

'Ellie, you're soaked!'

'Dominic, come out of there, you haven't got any wellies on!'

'Oh, Alexander, look how wet you are!'

'We'll have to turn round!' Ann announced to Finlay's relief. 'There's no way we can get the children through all this water. We'd better go to the other picnic area by the car park.'

There were choruses of disappointment from the children who were splashing in the water, but at last the adults got them all together and they headed safely back down the track.

I did it! thought Finlay in amazement. *I made them turn round!*

He pulled the shield down to his side and the magic barrier vanished. Immediately the waterfall began to fall as normal again. Finlay felt a rush of triumph. He'd turned the playgroup back down the mountain. He'd cast a really strong shield and managed to hold it in place. 'Go, me!' he muttered.

Then suddenly he remembered the Giant Boar. Was Max OK? He began to clamber across the rocks. But the effort of casting the shield had taken its toll. His head felt dizzy and his whole body seemed to ache. He felt like lying down and resting, but there was no time. He had to get back up the mountain as quickly as he could. Picking his bike up again Finlay forced his weary muscles into action. *I've got to get to Max*. The thought raced through his head as he cycled past Old John's Grave and into the trees. *Please, Max*, he thought desperately, *be all right . . .*

★

Max was still in the tree. The boar really was very stupid. It kept charging into things – trees and bushes – as if thinking they might be hiding another wild boar. It was getting angrier and angrier all the time.

Max watched as it charged headlong into a nearby clump of bramble bushes and ripped them apart with its tusks. A terrified rabbit bounded out. The boar spiked it on one of its tusks, then gulped it down in a single bite.

For a moment Max imagined what would happen to *him* if he fell out of the tree. He made another wild-boar sound, which sent the boar charging off round the clearing, and tried not to think about it.

'Max!'

Finlay was running through the trees, his face pale.

'Be careful!' Max yelled as the boar sighted Finlay. Its eyes lit up with a savage delight. Giving a high, throaty squeal it charged straight at him.

With a huge effort Finlay forced his tiredness away and threw the shield up. *I can do this*, he thought bravely. *I managed to move the waterfall. I can stop the boar too*. Hercules' shield felt strong and solid in his hand. Confidence surged through him. *Shield me!* he commanded in his head.

A silvery barrier swirled out, stopping in mid-air. It looked firm and unyielding.

The boar crashed into it, but the barrier didn't even tremble.

'Way to go, Fin!' Max exclaimed.

Using the barrier to cover him Finlay ran to the tree Max was in.

'Did you manage to stop the playgroup?' Max demanded as Finlay joined him in the branches.

Finlay nodded. 'I got the waterfall to fall on the path. They've gone to the picnic area by the car park.'

'That's great!' Max exclaimed.

The boar charged furiously at the tree.

'Hang on!' Max yelled, bracing himself for the impact, but the barrier held firm and the boar crashed back.

'This is cool!' Finlay said, beginning to enjoy his superpower for the first time. 'I think I'm beginning to get the hang of these magic barriers.'

'Yeah,' Max said. 'But I'm not sure how they're going to help us get the boar back to the castle.'

Finlay felt as if the waterfall had just doused him. He'd been so pleased to have stopped the playgroup and to have mastered the superpower he'd forgotten about the task they had to do that day.

'We can't stay up here forever,' Max went on. 'We've got to find a way of catching the boar.'

'But how?' Finlay said, looking down

at the rhino-sized beast with its bloodstained tusks.

'I dunno,' Max replied. 'Could we trap it? You know, in a cave or something?'

Finlay stared at him. 'Of course!' he exclaimed. 'We trap it. But not in a cave – in a pit!'

CHAPTER SIX

OLD JOHN'S GRAVE

'A pit?' Max echoed uncertainly. 'But won't it take ages to dig one?'

'We don't have to – we can use Old John's Grave!' Finlay pictured the deep pit near the top of the mountain that he'd just cycled past. 'It's perfect. We can chase the boar there by making lots of noise.'

'Yeah,' Max said eagerly. 'Hercules said it hates noise.'

'I can cast barriers to protect us,' Finlay went on excitedly. 'This might just work!'

Max frowned. 'But if we trap it in the pit, how are we going to get it to the castle? We have to get it back to the castle grounds to have completed the task.'

Finlay hesitated. Max had a point. 'We can deal with that later,' he said. 'Let's just trap it, then at least it can't charge around and hurt anyone else on the mountain. We can think of a way to get it to the castle later.'

Not hurting anyone sounded good. Max looked down at the boar. 'OK. So we jump down from the tree and chase it then?'

'Yeah, making lots of noise,' Finlay said.

Max took a deep breath. 'Now?'

'Yes,' Finlay said grimly. He met Max's eyes. 'Now!'

They both jumped from the tree together.

As Finlay leapt the magic shield vanished and the boar hurtled straight into the tree trunk, splitting it in two. Shaking its head, it got unsteadily to its feet. Blood dribbled from its snout.

'Quick, before it recovers!' Finlay said. Taking advantage of its confusion he began shouting, 'Go on! Go away! Scram!'

Max ran to his side and joined in with the shouting.

The boar hesitated and took a step backwards. 'Louder!' Finlay exclaimed. 'It doesn't like it!'

He and Max yelled as loudly as they could. Then suddenly the boar lifted its bleeding snout and scented the air. Its eyes lit up. The next instant it had swung round and begun to charge down the mountain.

'Is it running away from us?' Max demanded.

'Or has it just smelt something it wants for its lunch?' Finlay exclaimed.

He and Max pelted down the mountain. But there was no way they could keep pace with the Giant Boar at full gallop.

'We need our bikes!' Finlay said as they burst out of the trees on to the path. Jumping on their bikes, they pedalled as fast as they could. They could hear the boar as it charged on ahead of them down the path.

Finlay's heart raced. What if the boar really had smelt someone coming up the mountain? What if it killed someone?

Their bikes careered down the steep path. They were gaining on the boar fast.

'We need to turn it off this path!' Finlay yelled to Max. 'Let's overtake it.

I'll cast a shield to stop it then we can try and chase it through the trees towards the pit!'

'OK!' Max yelled back. 'Ready when you are!'

'Now!' Finlay shouted. 'Here goes!'

Ducking to avoid the clots of mud that the boar's feet were throwing up they managed to whizz past it.

Finlay leant back and slammed on his rear brake. His bike skidded to a stop. Half-falling off it, Finlay grabbed the shield from over his shoulder and thrust it out towards the boar.

Shield me! he thought desperately.

A disc shot out and covered the path. The boar charged into it and bounced back, falling into a heap. Max immediately began yelling at it. Finlay joined in. Jumping back on their bikes they began to cycle towards it. The boar got to its feet.

'Go on, you great lump of bacon!' Finlay yelled. 'Get lost!'

The boar hesitated and then scraped a front foot on the floor.

'Um, Finlay!' Max said, slowing down. 'It's not running!'

The boar gave a throaty growl and then charged towards them.

'It is now!' Finlay cried. 'Move it, Max!' Despite his terror, a small bit of his brain realized that cycling down the mountain and leading the boar straight towards the car park and other people was a very bad idea. Instead Finlay swung his bike into the trees.

He and Max pedalled for their lives as the Giant Boar thundered after them. It drew closer and closer. They could hear it snorting savagely, feel the pounding of its hooves, smell the stench of its hot breath . . .

'Fin! Watch out for the pit!' Max exclaimed as he saw Old John's Grave appearing in front of them.

An idea came to Finlay's mind. 'No, Max! Keep cycling and on the count of three, stop as fast as you can!' he cried. 'Trust me! One . . .'

The overgrown pit loomed up. The boar was right behind them.

'Two . . .'

They were almost on top of the pit – but the boar was almost on top of them. Finlay could hear its teeth snapping viciously at his back tyre.

'Three!' he yelled.

He and Max jammed on their back brakes and swung their weight to the side. Their bikes skidded sideways, stopping mere centimetres away from the edge of Old John's Grave, just like when Finlay tried to stop before the gate at his house.

The boar also tried to stop, but it was too late. Its heavy body carried it onward and, with an enraged roar, it hurtled towards the edge and crashed over it.

Panting, Max and Finlay got off their bikes and peered over the edge.

The pit was about four metres deep. The boar was getting to its feet, lashing out with its tusks at the sides, grunting in fury. Seeing the boys it tried to charge up the pit but the sides were too steep and it fell back.

'We've caught it!' Max exclaimed, looking down at the raging beast.

He and Finlay shakily high-fived.

The boar shrieked in rage.

Finlay threw his shoulders back. 'Hey, you oversized sack of sausages!' he yelled. 'Can't get us!' The boar threw itself at the sides of the pit again, grunting wildly.

'It's crazy!' Max said.

The boar reared up. 'Watch out!' Finlay yelled.

The boys jumped back with their bikes as the boar's tusks swept through the air. With a grunt it overbalanced and fell back heavily into the pit.

Crash!

There was a high-pitched squeal and then a sudden eerie silence.

Max and Finlay looked at each other. 'What's happened?' Max said uncertainly.

The silence continued.

'Maybe . . . maybe it's dead,' Finlay said.

'It can't be.' But Max didn't sound certain. He went cautiously to the edge of the pit and gasped.

'What is it?' Finlay demanded.

Max turned round. 'It's gone!'

'What? Vanished like the lion and river monster did when we completed the task?' Finlay asked eagerly. 'Maybe that means we've completed Juno's task! Maybe . . .'

'No,' Max interrupted. 'It's not vanished, Finlay. It's just gone. Look!'

Finlay joined him at the edge of the pit.

In the bottom was a gaping hole and the Giant Boar was nowhere to be seen!

CHAPTER SEVEN

FOLLOW THAT BOAR!

'It's fallen through that hole!' Finlay exclaimed.

'Where to?' Max said.

'We'd better find out!' Finlay scrambled down the sides of the pit, hanging on to the creepers and grass. 'If we lose it now we might never get it back to the castle in time.'

Max followed him. They went to the

edge of the hole at the bottom of the pit and, crouching down, looked in. There was a big dark area beneath them.

'Maybe it's an underground cave or something,' Max suggested.

'But if it's a cave, where's the boar?' Finlay frowned. Kneeling down he stuck his head right into the hole. 'It looks more like a passageway.'

Max looked into the hole too. 'Or a tunnel!'

'Hey! Maybe it's that tunnel Jasmine was talking about!' Finlay exclaimed. 'The one that leads from the castle to Saddleback Mountain.'

'Yeah! It . . . Argh!' Max broke off as suddenly the weakened ground they were kneeling on gave way. He and Finlay fell into the hole below. Shouting in alarm they crashed down on to a rocky floor. Dried mud and grass rained down on them.

Coughing and wiping the mud from his face Max sat up. 'You OK, Fin?'

Finlay tested his arms and legs – they still seemed to work. 'Yeah. How about you?'

'Think so.'

Finlay shook the dust from his hair and got to his feet. They were in a

wide, high tunnel that had been carved through the mountain. 'This *must* be the secret tunnel Jasmine was going on about,' he said. 'After hundreds of years – *we* found it!'

'Well, the boar found it really,' Max pointed out fairly.

'No way is some big pig getting the credit!' Finlay frowned. 'Where *is* the boar anyway?'

'Dunno. Maybe it's run away.' Max tried to get his bearings. 'The castle must be that way,' he said, pointing to the right.

'So the other entrance – the one into the mountains – must be this way,' Finlay said, looking to the left. 'I guess it's blocked up or people would have noticed it.'

Max looked up. The hole they had fallen through was a couple of metres above them and the sides of the rocky tunnel were very smooth with no obvious hand or footholds. 'Er, Fin? How are we going to get out of here?'

They looked at each other.

'Let me get this straight,' Finlay said slowly. 'We're stuck in a tunnel with no way out and there's a giant boar with razor-sharp tusks somewhere nearby.'

'A giant boar with razor-sharp tusks who's very, very angry with the two boys who've chased it halfway across a mountain.' Max gulped.

'This is not good. Not good at all,' Finlay whispered.

'We need to get out of here!' Max frantically started trying to find some handholds on the wall, but couldn't get a grip on the smooth rock at all.

'What's that noise?' Finlay swung round. Down the passageway to the right came the faint but unmistakable sound of grunting.

'The boar's coming!' Max said. 'It must have gone that way and turned back. Quick!'

They tried climbing the wall but it was no use. There really was no way out!

Finlay wracked his brains. 'I've got the shield and superpower still. I can try and protect us.'

'But for how long?' said Max. 'You'll get tired in the end, the barrier will get weaker, and then . . .' His voice trailed off. 'Let's make a run for it before the boar sees us!' he said quickly. 'We just need to stay alive until sunset and then the boar will vanish!'

'Along with any chance of saving Hercules,' said Fin bitterly. 'Or . . . hey, hang on!' His eyes lit up. 'Of course! We do have to run. But not *away* from the boar. Towards it!'

Max frowned. 'Have you gone mental?'

'Don't you see?' Finlay said urgently. 'We've got to *chase* the boar back towards the castle! If we can get it back to the castle grounds it will disappear. We'll have completed the task!' The grunting was echoing down the tunnel now and the boys could hear the loud thundering of the boar's feet on the stone as it came closer.

'But, Fin!' Max said. 'It's not exactly been running away from us so far!'

'I know but you could tell it didn't really like us making all that noise on the mountain,' Finlay said. 'It did stop it for a few moments, and down here,' he looked round at the tunnel, 'our voices will really echo, so the noise we make will be much louder.'

Max hesitated. 'It might work.'

'It *has* to!' Finlay said grimly.

At that very moment the boar came steaming round the corner. Its huge bulk bore down on Max and Finlay like a runaway train. As its piggy eyes spotted them it gave a crazed squeal. Opening its mouth to reveal its jagged teeth it increased its speed.

'Charge!' Finlay yelled.

Max gave up thinking and ran side by side with Finlay towards the boar, shouting as loudly as he could. A look of confusion crossed the boar's face. It definitely hadn't expected the boys to run towards it. It began to slow down.

'Shield me!' gasped Finlay, holding the shield out in front of him. A barrier swirled into the air between them and the boar.

The boar seemed to be learning about the magic barriers. It skidded to a halt, bumping its swollen snout into the unyielding surface. It staggered backwards, shaking its head.

'More noise!' Finlay exclaimed.

The boys yelled even louder. Their voices echoed through the rocky tunnel, bouncing off all the walls and rebounding. The boar took a step backwards, its ears twitching. Finlay began banging the shield as well. Max saw a loose rock on the floor and began banging it against the wall.

The boar looked over its shoulder and then back at the two yelling boys.

'Let's run at it again!' Max suggested.

Finlay held up the shield and they ran forward, shouting.

Suddenly the boar decided enough was enough. It didn't like these two boys with their shimmering circle, these boys who did strange things like running towards it instead of running away and who made such a loud, horrible noise. Its brain wasn't big enough to cope. The savage desire to destroy faded from its eyes and it did the only thing it could think of. It turned tail and ran.

'Hooray!' Max and Finlay cheered, racing after it.

The boar galloped down the tunnel with the boys close behind it. On and on they went until Max and Finlay had stitches in their sides. Finlay used the magic shield to prod the boar along; every time it touched the boar's hindquarters, the boar squealed and galloped faster. Luckily the shimmering of the magic shield also cast some light, so they could see where they were going.

'Look up ahead, Max!' Finlay gasped.

In the distance something was

blocking the tunnel. As they got closer they could see it was a large rockfall. Faint gleams of light shone through the cracks in the stones.

'It must be the entrance!' Max exclaimed. 'The boar's heading straight for it!'

'It's not going to stop!' Finlay yelled.

The boar charged at the rockfall. Max was filled with an awful thought. 'Oh no! What if we were wrong and the tunnel doesn't come out in the castle?' he said.

Finlay felt sick. 'What if it comes out somewhere in the village?'

'Or by the car park?' Max cried.

They looked at each other. 'It's too late to stop it now!' Finlay gasped.

CHAPTER EIGHT

LIGHTNING BOLTS!

The boar smashed into the rockfall like a hairy torpedo. The stones exploded, flying everywhere. With a squeal of triumph the boar burst into the light . . . and vanished into thin air!

Max and Finlay raced to the hole and looked out.

They were in the castle keep!

The tunnel entrance had been hidden by a section of the castle's walls that had collapsed long ago.

'We did it!' Max shouted. 'We got the boar back!'

They clambered out of the hole.

'It's really gone!' Finlay said in relief.

An angry shriek rang out and a hawk swooped down. As it landed on the grass it magically transformed into Juno. A cloak of brown-grey feathers swirled around her. She looked to be in a towering rage. 'No!' she exclaimed, raising her hands.

Acting instinctively Finlay held out the shield. 'Shield me!' he cried.

He was just in time. As a lightning bolt fired through the air from the goddess's hands, a magic barrier formed.

The lightning bolt hit it with a bright flash and bounced away into the sky.

'Your luck holds out, it seems,' Juno snarled. She lowered her hands and strode towards them.

Max and Finlay shrank back. Until now, Juno had never tried to injure them directly. But then they'd never seen her looking so angry before.

She stopped and glared at them. 'So you have completed another task,' she said icily. 'And another power returns to Hercules.'

Finlay felt a warm swirling in his chest. Suddenly a golden light flooded out of him. It streamed across the keep towards the tower. As it hit the inside wall, it disappeared. The shield in Finlay's hand vanished and the bricks around Hercules' face began to crumble away.

'You did it, boys!' he exclaimed as he looked out. 'My power has returned!' His hair had lost its streaks of grey and he seemed to be standing taller. With every power that returned to him he seemed to grow in strength and stature. 'But what of the little children?'

'They're all OK.' Finlay looked warily at Juno. She glared at him but made no movement with her hands. Skirting her, Finlay ran across the grass to the tower. Max hastily joined him. 'We managed to stop the boar.'

'Well, we made lots of noise and used our bikes and the shield and . . .'

The words tumbled out of the boys. Hercules looked more and more astonished as they told him how they had managed to get the boar back to the castle. 'I am amazed,' he told them. 'You do not act in the accepted ways of heroes. You use strange methods and you are both impetuous . . .'

Finlay looked at Max. Max was better at long words than he was.

'We don't think before we do stuff,' Max translated.

'But despite this you manage to achieve everything real heroes would.'

Hercules looked from one to the other. 'Or maybe it is *because* of this,' he added softly.

Max and Finlay glanced at each other.

'Do you think he's trying to tell us we're crazy?' Finlay grinned.

Max grinned back. 'He could be right!'

There was a loud clap of thunder. The boys jumped and swung round. Juno strode across the keep. 'Do not be fooled! You will not succeed again!' she said. 'Tomorrow you will face the Man-Eating Birds of Stymphalia. They are vicious and super-intelligent and work together to hunt down their prey.' A dangerous smile lit up her face. 'And just think, in the morning, their prey will be you!'

'You cannot make them face the

Stymphalian Birds!' Hercules exclaimed. 'You . . .'

Juno clapped her hands and the stones immediately closed over his face, cutting him off.

'I thought I told you I can do anything I like, Hercules!' She laughed evilly. 'Until tomorrow! She clapped her hands again. As a bolt of lightning forked to the ground in the centre of the castle the boys blinked. When they opened their eyes Juno was gone. There was just a hawk flying up into the air.

'So it's birds tomorrow,' Max said, trying to stop his voice from shaking. 'Man-eating birds.'

'At least birds don't have teeth and tusks,' Fin pointed out. 'We'll win Hercules his next power back!'

'Yeah, we will!' Max agreed, feeling better.

Finlay's stomach rumbled loudly. 'I'm starving. Let's go and get our bikes and go home.' He shot Max a sideways look. 'I want a bacon sandwich.'

Max grinned. 'Bangers and mash for me.'

'Followed by trotter-flavoured ice cream?' Finlay suggested.

'I *scream*, more like . . .' Max said.

Laughing together, Max and Finlay headed out of the castle.

Overhead, a hawk hovered. It screamed furiously and then sped away until it became just a black dot in the blue sky.

ABOUT THE AUTHOR

ALEX CLIFF LIVES IN A VILLAGE IN LEICESTERSHIRE, NEXT DOOR TO FIN AND JUST DOWN THE ROAD FROM MAX, BUT UNFORTUNATELY THERE IS NO CASTLE ON THE OUTSKIRTS OF THE VILLAGE. ALEX'S HOME IS FILLED WITH TWO CHILDREN AND TWO LARGE AND VERY SLOBBERY PET MONSTERS.

puffin.co.uk

CAN MAX AND FIN DEFEAT MAN-EATING BIRDS?

FIND OUT IN . . .

DID YOU KNOW?

Hercules lived in Ancient Greece. He was the son of a woman named Alcmene and the god Zeus. When Hercules was a baby he could fight snakes with his bare hands! The labours he had to complete were originally set for him by his cousin Eurystheus, King of Mycenae.

THE ERYMANTHIAN BOAR

This was a ferocious beast that attacked people and destroyed everything in its path. When Hercules first fought it he had to look for it on the Mountain of Erymanthus and chase it from its hiding place. Unlike some of his other labours, he had to capture this beast alive and take it to Mycenae in chains.

puffin.co.uk

YOUR SUPER POWERS QUEST

YOU NEED:

2 players
2 counters
1 dice
and nerves of steel!

YOU MUST:

Collect all **seven** superpowers and save Hercules, who has been trapped in the castle by the evil goddess, Juno. All you have to do is roll the dice and follow the steps on the books – try not to land on Juno's rock or one of the monsters!

YOU CAN:

PLAY BOOK BY BOOK

The game is only complete when all seven books in the series are lined up. But if you don't have them all yet, you can still complete the quests! Whoever lands on the 'GO' rock first is the winner of that particular quest.

PLAY THE WHOLE GAME

Whoever collects all seven superpowers and is first to land on the final rock has completed the entire quest and saved Hercules!

REMEMBER:

If you land on a 'Back to the Start' symbol, don't worry – you don't have to go all the way back to book one – just back to the start of the game on the book you are playing.

GOOD LUCK, SUPERHEROES!

puffin.co.uk